DIVINE

STORY OF A HERO

ARCHISHMAN PANDEY

BlueRose Publishers

First Published in March 2019

ISBN: 978-93-5347-299-3

BLUE ROSE PUBLISHERS
www.bluerosepublishers.com
info@bluerosepublishers.com
+91 8882 898 898

Cover Design:
Srijan Bandyopadhyay

Typographic Design:
Tanya Raj Upadhyay

Editor:
Shreya

Distributed by: Blue Rose, Amazon, Flipkart, Shopclues

Divine:
The Story of a Hero

Contents

Chapter 1

In the beginning there was nothing. Out of this nothingness erupted two individuals: Purity and Chaos. Purity symbolized everything pure about the cosmos and Chaos represented the evil.

Purity created planets and brought people to life, whereas Chaos destroyed planets and brought them to dust; this ensured that the universe was balanced.

This process continued for several millennia until Chaos grew impatient. His strength increased and he started destroying more than one planet at a time.

When Purity began to notice this, she was outraged. She felt the cosmos heading towards Chaos. This was when she broke the agreement.

Both Chaos and Purity had had an agreement that they would never produce kids, or as they called it: *miniature replicas* of themselves.

Having broken the agreement, Purity made one out of the positive force inside her and named him *Phoenix*. He was a representation of all the good that was left in the Cosmos.

Chaos started feeling the strange aura of Phoenix, so he went to the planet known as Earth, or Planet 44309. There he created two souls to oppose Phoenix. Neither of them had powers similar to that of Chaos, but they were strong.

When Chaos saw that his creations were nothing but weak, he sought to create another that would be as powerful as him. The new one had the exact powers as Chaos himself.

Over time, Chaos weakened. For the first time in history, he was overtaken by Purity. Purity saw this as the perfect moment to cast a spell older than both herself and Chaos and banish them both to their birthplace.

She did this, not knowing about Chaos's creations that prevailed on Earth. Purity was banished along with her replica but the replicas of chaos roamed free. The universe was in peace for several million years after that.

But then…

All hell broke loose on Earth and even in exile, Chaos began to grow stronger. Purity saw no way but to release her creation to Earth.

She created a breach point in their birthplace and launched Phoenix to Earth. She did this hoping that it would control the evil on Earth. Phoenix lost his way many a times during his journey to Earth.

He visited many a universe and saw everything. He basically grew up in that journey. He saw the greatest light and the greatest darkness. All of this seemed to bow to him and lead him to Earth.

By the time he finally reached Earth, his appearance had changed; he was now a grown man with a big beard and pure white eyes. He had electricity all around him.

He was attended by a large crowd of people during his crash. Phoenix suddenly seemed to know their names and language.

He asked those people, "What year is this and where am I?"

"Oh boy! You seem peculiar," the people replied. "What is this year thing you mentioned? Is it some kind of ancient force? For the answer of the second part, you are in the home of the children of Chaos."

Phoenix wasn't foolish. Although he didn't know Chaos, he knew this was something very bad.

The more Phoenix thought, the more he forgot. He asked those men whether he could have some shelter for the night. The men thought for a while and then the person who seemed the eldest replied, “Yes, you can.”

Phoenix went to their secret cave. It was made out of stone. Phoenix thought about the various planets he had seen. Those were much more advanced and prosperous. Phoenix thought all he could about who had sent him and why, but the only thing he remembered about that was a bright white light.

As Phoenix was getting ready to sleep, he suddenly remembered his quest. A voice spoke in his mind, “You are on Earth to defend the good and *annihilate* the evil; you are planet 44309’s last hope.”

He spoke to the people about this but they thought that he was just hallucinating. Whilst the other people slept like the dead, Phoenix kept hearing voices. These voices seemed to be inviting Phoenix, but he just didn’t know where.

Out of curiosity, Phoenix followed the voices. He saw a hole just between the cave and the cave’s exit.

Phoenix glanced at the other side of the hole and what he saw was extraordinary. He saw a planet way more advanced. They had a rainbow bridge.

A weird looking guy with orange eyes was standing in front of him. He said to him, "I am Heimdall. Phoenix, you are welcome to Asgard."

Chapter 2

His first reaction was like 'okay, do I go back now or what?' Heimdall was taking him to what looked like a palace. On it was written 'Welcome to the home of Odin.' If the people had not been so gloomy, it would have been a wonderful place.

On the throne there sat a person. He had a great beard and tensed eyes. Phoenix thought that this must be Odin, the ruler. He looked like someone who was going to fight in a huge war. Odin's eyes were changing color every second. For a second, he seemed to have yellow eyes and the next he had grey eyes.

Odin was deeply engrossed in some work, but suddenly looked up and saw Phoenix. He started speaking, "Hi Phoenix, you've crash-landed on our planet today, but it's a good thing that you did. I sense many abilities in you. We on Asgard have a very difficult situation.

Ragnarok, that signifies the end of our deities and race, is upon us. I have a very important mission for you. I, Odin, Allfather, want to change Asgard's destiny. I want you to go to Muspleheim and end Surt and his kind, and after that, destroy Loki's ship and kill him."

"Wait, what?! What is Muspleheim? And who is this Loki and where can I find him?" Phoenix said to Odin.

Odin replied, "I am in a hurry and can't explain it to you, but my son Thor will."

A dark figure with a hammer emerged from the shadows. He was very dirty; it seemed like he hadn't had a bath in centuries. "Of course father, leave it to me," Thor said.

Odin left his seat and quickly teleported out of there. Thor said to Phoenix, "I should show you to your room, then I will tell you about the history of the nine realms, and your quest, since I am your partner."

Phoenix was smiling on the outside but on the inside, he was thinking 'I would rather go alone than with this goat.'

Thor accompanied Phoenix to his room and told him that Pheonix was going to attend a feast, but Phoenix replied, "I don't want to attend a feast; I just want to do the work and get back to Earth."

Thor said to him, "As you wish," then began explaining everything:

"Yggdrasil is a tree that connects the nine worlds. The gods go to Yggdrasil daily to assemble into their traditional governing assemblies. The branches of Yggdrasil extend far into the heavens and the tree is supported by three roots that extend far away into other locations.

"There are nine planets that are connected to Yggdrasil—

"Asgard, the home of the Aesir ruled by the god Odin

"Alfheim, the home of the light elves

"Nidaveller, the home of the dwarves

"Midgard, the home of humans

"Jotunheim, the home of the giant

"Vanaheim, the home of the Vanir

"Nifleheim, a world of ice and snow

"Muspleheim, a world of fire and lava, and home of the Surt

"Helheim, the home of the dishonourable dead, ruled by the Goddess Hel

"There were also many ancient monsters that dwelled in the deepest locations.

"There was man called Ymir. He brought winters that were endless, so he was killed by Odin. His descendants grew angry and discovered the ancient prophecy of Ragnarok. We grow helpless now as it is about to begin in three days and it means our end.

"According to the prophecy, the wolves Skoll and Hati, who have hunted the sun and moon through the skies since the beginning of time, will at last catch their prey.

"The stars too, will disappear, leaving nothing but a black void in the heavens. Yggdrasil, the great tree that holds the cosmos together, will tremble, and all the trees and even the mountains will fall to the ground.

"The chain that has been holding back the monstrous wolf Fenrir will snap, and the beast will run free.

"Jormungand, the mighty serpent who dwells at the bottom of the ocean and encircles the land, will rise from the depths, spilling the seas over all the Earth as he makes land fall. These convulsions will shake the ship Naglfar free from its moorings.

"This ship, which is made from the fingernails and toenails of dead men and women will sail easily over the flooded Earth. Its crew will be an army of giants, the forces of Chaos and destruction, and its captain will be none other than Loki, the traitor to the gods, who will have broken free of the chains in which we had bound him.

"Fenrir, with fire blazing in his eyes and nostrils, will run across the Earth with his lower jaw on the ground and his upper jaw against the top of the sky, devouring everything in his path. Jormungand will spit his venom over all the world; poisoning land, water, and air alike.

"The dome of the sky will be split, and from the crack shall emerge the fire-giants from Muspleheim. Their leader shall be Surt, with a flaming sword brighter than the sun in his hand. As they march across Bifrost, the rainbow bridge to Asgard, the home of the gods, the bridge will break and fall behind them. An ominous horn blast will ring out; this will be Heimdall, the divine sentry, blowing the gjallerhorn to announce the arrival of the moment the gods have feared. Odin will anxiously consult the head of Mimir, the wisest of all beings, for counsel.

"The gods will decide to go to battle, even though they know what the prophecies have foretold concerning the outcome of this clash. They will arm themselves and meet their enemies on a battlefield called Vigrid.

"Odin will fight Fenrir and by his side will be the einherjar, the host of his chosen human warriors whom he has kept in Valhalla for just this moment. Odin and the champions of men will fight more valiantly than anyone has ever fought before. But it will not be enough. Fenrir will swallow Odin and his men. Then one of Odin's sons, Vidar, burning with rage, will charge the beast to avenge his father.

"On one of his feet will be the shoe that has been crafted for this very purpose; it has been made from all the scraps of leather that human shoemakers have ever discarded, and with-it Vidar will hold open the monster's mouth. Then he will stab his sword through the wolf's throat, killing him.

"Another wolf, Garm, and the god Tyr will slay each other.

"Heimdall and Loki will do the same, putting a final end to the trickster's treachery, but costing the gods one of their best in the process. The god Frey and the giant Surt will also be the end of each other. I and Jormungand, those age-old foes, will both finally have their chance to kill the other.

"I will succeed in felling the great snake with the blows of my hammer, but the serpent will have covered me in so much venom that I will not be able to stand for much longer; I will take nine paces before falling dead myself and adding my blood to the already-saturated soil of Vigrid.

"Then the remains of the world will sink into the sea, and there will be nothing left but the void. The creation and all that has occurred since will be completely undone, as if it had never happened."

Phoenix thought that this obviously wasn't *all* of creation since he had seen many other planets on his way to Earth. "So basically, I need to kill Surt, the leader of fire giants and then kill Loki? Cool. When do we get started?"

"Whenever you want little boy," Thor replied.

"Let's start then. And by the way, I am neither little nor a boy," Phoenix said.

Thor said, "Grab onto me and I will transport us to Muspleheim—our first stop. We need to kill Surt."

Chapter 3

Phoenix thought that the flight would be easy since he had flown a long way to Earth, but it wasn't. Thor's hammer was super uncomfortable, but it was the only way to get to Muspleheim. Phoenix's thoughts were wandering elsewhere. He was not thinking of the mission ahead, but the future.

He tried to get these thoughts out of his mind, but it was too late; they had already landed on Muspleheim.

There was fire everywhere, but Phoenix wasn't affected by it. He was somehow immune to it.

Thor said to him, "Do you have a plan? As I certainly don't."

Phoenix looked as if he was about to hit Thor on his face, but he calmed himself down and said to him, "We march through the front door, kill all the guards, and then Surt himself."

Thor replied, "Now that's a plan worthy of me; let's go!"

Both of them started walking. Phoenix started wondering whether he could summon that electricity that he'd had when he'd just landed on Earth. He tried to summon some, but only his hands lighted up with the electricity.

Both Thor and Phoenix had reached the door. Thor asked Phoenix to open it since he wanted to save his strength for Surt. Phoenix summoned his lightning and shot at the door; the door broke into pieces.

Thor stared at him in amazement and said, "That was simply amazing; even I, the god of lightning, can't produce that much power in my lightning. My lightning isn't strong enough to break the doors of Surt, but yours are. I wonder what is its source..."

Phoenix wasn't even listening to whatever Thor was saying; he was actually focused on locating the enemies in the room ahead of them.

Phoenix and Thor walked forward into the room. They could not find any fire giants, but then, all of a sudden, they were surrounded. A few of the fire giants had surrounded them.

Both Thor and Phoenix were ready to attack, but the fire giants spoke first: "Thor, son of Odin, and Phoenix, son of...interesting, very interesting. Phoenix, you're a powerful person; I will leave your introduction at that.

I am Overseeker; I can see everyone's worst memories and learn their origins in a minute; everyone's except yours, Phoenix. I have a proposal: submit yourself to Surt and both of you will be spared until Ragnarok."

Thor was going to pick up his hammer, but a plan formed in Phoenix's mind. Phoenix thought that getting captured would definitely earn them an appearance before Surt. Phoenix said to the fire giants, "We accept your gracious offer."

Thor was angry at Phoenix. Phoenix thought that Thor would understand why he had accepted the offer of getting arrested. Thor just couldn't get the plan inside his head.

They were taken through a very bright fire that blinded them.

Then, they reached the room where a single fire giant was sitting. Both Thor and Phoenix singled him out to be Surt. The room wasn't as empty as Phoenix thought it was.

There was an army of fire giants around the room. Surt spoke loudly enough for everyone in the room to hear:

"We have two people amongst us who have come here to kill me. They think they can stop Ragnarok. None of them know about the greater threat that we mean to stop. The destruction of the gods will give us the power to stop it."

Phoenix cleverly said to Surt, "And we will kill you." Phoenix broke through his barriers and so did Thor.

Both of them started lighting people up and blasting them. Phoenix gave a huge thunder-shock to the room and killed most of the fire giants in there.

When Phoenix looked around the corner to see Thor, all he saw was his hammer lying there. He saw that Thor was being smashed by Surt.

He was going to make a move and save Thor when Surt said to him, "You are one brave kid, aren't you? Ragnarok has already started; Loki's ship has reached Asgard. You can't stop it and neither can you stop Thor from dying."

Surt started to smash Thor's head, but then Phoenix screamed, "No!" He turned purple and released a power that he had not known about. He focused it on Surt.

When the power hit Surt, Surt exploded. Thor was on the floor but he managed to get up and say only two words, "Save Asgard." Phoenix managed to pick up Thor's hammer and start a portal back to Asgard.

Back at Asgard, the gods had tied up Loki and were about to kill him. Phoenix was surprised since this was not how the prophecy had predicted it. Phoenix asked Odin, "How is this even possible?"

Odin replied, "None of the fire giants showed up. Surt didn't show up. Frey didn't die. He called in peace and most warriors were disarmed. Fenrir died. Jormungand was killed by the Einherjar. All of humanity was saved. However, this isn't the end. We sense a greater evil coming; something that we will figure out. In the meantime, I want you to discover your true heritage. You are something I have never seen. You are powerful and unknown. Come on, I know exactly the place to go to."

Phoenix said to Odin, "Even Surt had said something like this. He had said that that there was a greater evil coming and destroying the gods would be the only way."

Odin thought for a while, then said, "Let's go Phoenix. Come on, follow me."

Chapter 4

Phoenix did as Odin said and followed him. He kept following him tell he came to an abrupt stop.

He was standing in front of a cave. Odin said, "This is the cave of the first two people that were created on Earth. They have even greater knowledge than me. If they decide to help you, you can finally be your true self. Just go inside the cave and follow the markings."

Phoenix was feeling fearless at the moment and ventured into the cave. Inside the cave, there were various markings. There were also two entities. One entity had come to Earth and created these.

These markings made Phoenix feel like something was stirring inside of him. He ventured further into the tunnel.

At the very end, he saw a fire. Besides the fire, there sat two people.

Phoenix thought that these must be the ancient people. They seemed to be meditating. Phoenix very slowly walked towards them.

As soon as Phoenix went towards them, the two men opened their eyes.

They looked at Phoenix and saw his white eyes and then bowed down to him. They said, "Welcome to Earth, son of Purity."

Phoenix looked startled and asked them, "What do you mean by 'son of Purity?' I just want to know who I am and why am I here."

The ancient spoke, "Sit down. We will explain everything to you."

The other ancient said, "I hope that you have read the signs and understood that there existed two entities." Phoenix nodded.

The first ancient said, "When Chaos overtook Purity, Purity made you as a hope for humanity. Chaos, who got greedy after your creation, first created us. We were to serve as his minions. Then, he created something else: something more powerful than us; something, that would rival you. Purity banished Chaos, and to maintain order, banished herself as well. She took you with her. The whereabouts of Chaos's son are unknown, but he is heading here, to Earth. You are the only one who can stop him."

Phoenix said, "I nearly failed to stop Ragnarok; how am I supposed to stop a greater evil coming my way?"

Both of them looked at each other, and then spoke together, "Remember yourself, first and only son of Purity, made from the pure in the universe, master of light, master of cosmic forces. Remember your destiny, remember your powers!"

Phoenix started floating in the air. He was turning, regaining his powers.

He turned white with the powers of the elements. Then he flew out of the cave with a speeds more than that of light.

He went to where Odin was waiting. Odin was surprised upon seeing him.

Phoenix said to Odin, "I have seen your future. It is in grave danger. If the upcoming calamity is not defeated, there may be no Planet 44309."

Chapter 5

Odin was stressed enough after the Ragnarok, but this had certainly made it worse. Odin immediately called a council of gods and by his side stood the one who possibly controlled him, Phoenix.

Phoenix had just been reminded of his true, ancient powers. He had come to accept that he was the only one who could stop his brother.

When the gods entered, they were in a celebratory mood. But when they entered the hall, they entered silently because of the presence of Phoenix.

Only Thor had the nerves to speak. He said, "What has happened father? Phoenix, why are you flying and why do you appear so white? Have you figured out the source of your thunder?"

Odin ignored Thor's questions and said to all the gods, "I, or more accurately Phoenix, ventured into the cave of the ancestors today. He received a prophecy that another, greater evil is coming. It predates even the ancestors. We must prepare for war and hope that Phoenix will lead us well."

Many people raised their eyebrows at his speech. Heimdall politely asked Odin, "Why should we trust Phoenix?"

Odin replied, "we shall trust him because he predates us, the ancestors, and the greater evil. We all know Purity. Phoenix is all that is pure because he is the first and only son of Purity, the creator. He holds powers that none of us have or will ever get."

Heimdall raised his objections again, "if he is the supreme, can he prove it?"

Odin got up to answer, but Phoenix stopped him in the air. Phoenix replied, "I think this is a good example. For your question Thor, I create lightning and I know no limits."

Phoenix then unfroze Odin and continued, "My brother, the son of he who created you all, of Chaos, is coming to destroy Earth. You must gather every bit of strength you have while I gather some information."

All of the gods departed from the hall, one by one. Heimdall tried to see the enemy but Phoenix said, "It is of no use Heimdall; he hides himself using ancient magic."

Heimdall stopped trying and went to prepare for battle.

Whilst the gods were preparing, Phoenix slipped away into a cave. He sat down there and tried to reach his mother. He only got glimpses of her.

While focusing on her voice, he heard it as if she was speaking to him now.

The voice said, "Phoenix, he is closer than you think he is. He is right next to Planet 44309. Get ready immediately. You have grown wise and strong. I must go now, before Chaos comes back."

Phoenix flew out of the cave and went out of Earth's atmosphere. Phoenix saw him—a great black light rushing towards Earth, or rather, him. Phoenix closed his eyes once and then opened it back. He was being attacked.

He was flown across the atmosphere of Earth and punched continuously, but Phoenix managed to summon some lightning and get rid of him and fly back to Asgard.

He went to the Bifrost, where all the armies were standing. He said to them, "He is here, brace yourselves."

Chapter 6

Phoenix was flying in front of the army, commandeering them.

Then he came: Chaos's son. He halted in front of the army and lowered his hood. He looked exactly like Phoenix, except everything in him was black. He shouted, "I see, you have gathered the weaklings, the failures. I am going to finish you first and then these weaklings. I suppose you all know who I am. I am Jackius, Chaos's heir."

Phoenix yelled loudly, "Charge!"

It all commenced. All of the Asgardians aimed their best at Jackius, but it didn't work. Only Thor managed to make a scratch. Jackius blasted all of them as if they were ants. Then he came for Phoenix.

Jackius dragged him along the surface of the Earth, hitting him hard with all his powers. Phoenix couldn't fight back, but he figured out a way. He made a ball of all the elements and blasted it towards Jackius. Then Phoenix hit him with the biggest thunder ever.

Jackius protected himself with a shield made up of the all the evil on the Earth. Phoenix then directly flew at Jackius with all his might and punched him. His shield broke and he started bleeding like a mortal. This angered Jackius.

Jackius knew how to make weapons using dark magic and started making orbs and a big armour. He was throwing it all at Phoenix. Whilst Phoenix was distracted, Jackius covered Phoenix with darkness and then attacked him.

Phoenix felt tired; he had tried every trick in the book.

Jackius was about to kill Phoenix when a hammer made him lose his balance. Jackius saw Thor, the only Asgardian left, making his move.

Jackius made Thor fly and then destroyed him. Phoenix screamed, "No!"

This gave Phoenix enough time to make his move. Phoenix punched Jackius with lightning. He made him fall to the core of the Earth through his punches.

Jackius just didn't seem to die. Jackius always regrouped. That is when Phoenix remembered those purple powers. He summoned those powers with the help of his anger and let it loose on Jackius.

Jackius was destroyed but his evilness kept him together. Phoenix then plucked a leaf out of Jackius's book. He concentrated on all the good in the universe and then blasted it at Jackius. Jackius was then truly destroyed.

Phoenix rose up to the surface of the Earth and all he saw was damage.

Chapter 7

Phoenix saw that all of the Asgardians were dead.

Thor was nowhere to be seen, but Phoenix also presumed him dead because of the blast of Jackius.

He repaired as much damage as he could. He conducted burials for all the Asgardians and turned them into stars in our galaxy. Phoenix saw the damage that he and Jackius had made. He was no better than him.

He shouted to himself, "Mother, I have failed you! I sought out peace, but brought only Chaos. I have defied the one thing that you stand for; I have defied my true identity. I know no way now. I am here, stranded on this planet, without any friends, all alone. What shall I do?"

Phoenix stood there on his knees. There seemed to be no way. No one had got out of this mess that he had created.

Right about then, a bright light flashed through the sky and teleported him. He was teleported to another planet. This planet seemed greener and lonelier than Earth, or rather, the Earth that he had initially arrived at.

There was not a single person to be seen.

Phoenix seemed to feel that this planet was more powerful at its core than Earth. Then, he saw a person.

The person zoomed towards him and picked him up. Phoenix seemed to recognize this person.

Phoenix had never seen a person who was like him. Then he realized who that person was, and where he was.

Phoenix managed to say, "Mother, is this you?"

The person smiled and said, "Welcome Home Phoenix, my son."

www.ingramcontent.com/pod-product-compliance
Ingram Content Group UK Ltd.
Pitfield, Milton Keynes, MK11 3LW, UK
UKHW042001190726
13854UKWH00005B/2111

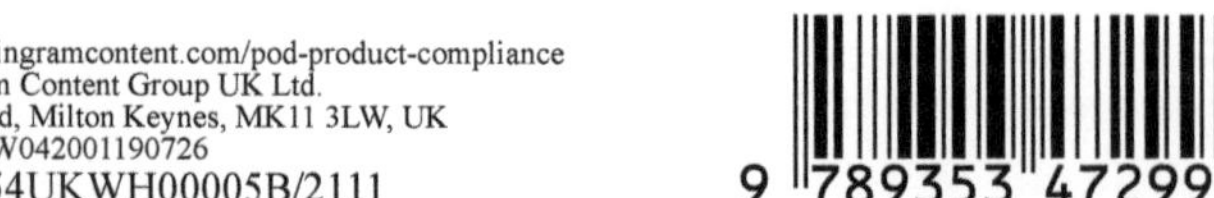